SEA LIFE SECRETS

HARDY BOYS

→Clue Book←

#12

SEA LIFE SECRETS

BY FRANKLIN W. DIXON ↔ ILLUSTRATED BY SANTY GUTIÉRREZ

ALADDIN

NEW YORK   LONDON   TORONTO   SYDNEY   NEW DELHI

This book is a work of fiction. Any references to historical events, real people, or real places are used fictitiously. Other names, characters, places, and events are products of the author's imagination, and any resemblance to actual events or places or persons, living or dead, is entirely coincidental.

ALADDIN

An imprint of Simon & Schuster Children's Publishing Division
1230 Avenue of the Americas, New York, NY 10020
First Aladdin paperback edition August 2020
Text copyright © 2020 by Simon & Schuster, Inc.
Illustrations copyright © 2020 by Santy Gutiérrez
Also available in an Aladdin hardcover edition.

For information about special discounts for bulk purchases, please contact
Simon & Schuster Special Sales at 1-866-506-1949 or business@simonandschuster.com.
The Simon & Schuster Speakers Bureau can bring authors to your live event.
For more information or to book an event contact the Simon & Schuster Speakers Bureau
at 1-866-248-3049 or visit our website at www.simonspeakers.com.
Series designed by Karina Granda
Cover designed by Tiara Iandiorio
The text of this book was set in Adobe Garamond Pro.
Manufactured in the United States of America 0720 OFF
2 4 6 8 10 9 7 5 3 1
Library of Congress Cataloging-in-Publication Data
Names: Dixon, Franklin W., author. | Gutiérrez, Santy, 1971- illustrator.
Title: Sea life secrets / by Franklin W. Dixon ; illustrated by Santy Gutiérrez.
Description: First Aladdin hardcover edition. | New York : Aladdin, [2020] | Series: Hardy Boys
clue book ; 12 | Audience: Ages 6-9. | Summary: Detective brothers Frank and Joe Hardy are
on the case when a sea star goes missing during their school field trip to the Bayport Aquarium.
Identifiers: LCCN 2020016075 (print) | LCCN 2020016076 (ebook) |
ISBN 9781534442580 (paperback) | ISBN 9781534442597 (hardcover) |
ISBN 9781534442603 (ebook)
Subjects: CYAC: Aquariums—Fiction. | School field trips—Fiction. | Aquarium animals—
Fiction. | Penguins—Fiction. | Brothers—Fiction. | Mystery and detective stories.
Classification: LCC PZ7.D644 Sbm 2020 (print) | LCC PZ7.D644 (ebook) | DDC [Fic]—dc23
LC record available at https://lccn.loc.gov/2020016075

CONTENTS

SEA LIFE SECRETS

INTO THE DEEP

"Sea creatures rule!" nine-year-old Frank Hardy shouted, hopping off the school bus in front of the Bayport Aquarium.

"Follow me, kids! We don't want to be late for our tour of Tide Town!" Frank's science teacher, Ms. Klinger, called out as the rest of the Bayport Elementary School third and fourth graders joined the packed crowd in front of the aquarium.

A large banner above the entrance announced the

TIDE TOWN GRAND OPENING along with pictures of starfish, sea urchins, horseshoe crabs, rays, and some of the other creatures featured in the aquarium's brand-new touch pool exhibit.

"This is one of the coolest field trips ever!" Frank's younger brother, Joe, said, following Ms. Klinger and the other chaperones toward the banner. "I hope we get to touch a shark."

"I don't think the Tide

Town exhibit has any sharks, but it does have rays, and they're related to sharks." Frank pointed out the creature on the Tide Town banner. "They're kind of like flattened sharks, with fins that look like wings, and long, pointy tails."

"Sweet!" Joe pumped his fist. "I'm going to touch a shark's flattened cousin!"

"Rays, skates, and sharks are all members of the same group of fish called elasmobranch," a kid with curly hair, a neon-green T-shirt,

AND OPENING

and blue-framed glasses chimed in, pushing his way between Frank and Joe as they entered the aquarium. "They don't have bones like regular fish. Their skeletons are made out of cartilage instead. That's the same stuff as our noses!"

"I knew that," Frank mumbled.

Frank was one of Ms. Klinger's best science students, and there was only one classmate who could out-fact him when it came to marine biology: Brady Jordan. Brady carried a sketchbook filled with drawings of sea life in one hand and a lunch box designed to look just like a fish tank in the other.

"Speaking of rays, there's one now." Joe pointed to a six-foot-tall walking ray with a giant cartoon grin, taking pictures with kids from another school. "I didn't know they had legs, though."

"That's Reggie the Ray. He's one of the new mascots the aquarium unveiled for Tide Town's grand opening." Frank looked around the lobby. "There's another one named Seymour the Sea Star, but I don't see him. They're both named after real creatures in the exhibit."

"Hi, Reggie!" Joe called to the costumed mascot. Reggie waved back with one of his oversize wings. "I'm going to have a real ray and all kinds of other cool creatures as soon as I convince my parents to buy me a home aquarium," Brady boasted. "I might even make my own touch pool."

As the group followed the signs toward Tide Town, a classmate with a ponytail and wearing a T-shirt with a glittery green dragon on it dropped back to join the conversation.

"Your parents are still saying no, huh, Brady?" she asked. It wasn't any surprise that Brady wanted a home aquarium. He talked about it all the time.

"Oh. Hi, Mira. They're saying no for now, but if I bug them enough, they'll have to agree."

"Avery is totally obsessed with her fish tank." Mira frowned. "I wish she were here to see Tide Town too."

"It stinks that your sister had her tonsils out right before our field trip," Joe said. "Avery's the only other person at school who gets as excited about this marine bio stuff as Brady and my bro."

"Yeah, I don't love fish so much, but I do love my twin sis." Mira put her hands together to make a heart shape. "I'm going to find the best souvenir in the whole aquarium to bring home for her so she doesn't feel left out."

"How come you're not excited about Tide Town? Aren't twins supposed to like all the same things?" Brady asked.

"We're not *identical* twins. We don't even look the same. Even if we did, every twin has their own special personality. And I definitely won't be petting any slimy sea creatures." Mira shuddered. "I am excited to see the penguins, though. They're the cutest."

This time it was Brady who shuddered. "No thanks! My appreciation of sea life doesn't include flightless seabirds."

"But everybody likes penguins!" Frank insisted. "Ms. Klinger said we can explore on our own after Tide Town, and feeding time at the penguin exhibit is at the top of our list."

He pulled out a map of the aquarium and pointed to the outdoor penguin exhibit circled in orange marker. It was on the other side of the rain-forest exhibit on the level below Tide Town, circled in blue.

Brady started to turn red. "I'm—I'm afraid of penguins. It's a real phobia some people have."

"That's okay, Brady. Everybody's afraid of something." Joe put a friendly hand on Brady's shoulder as they walked past the entrance to Shark Row. "Like me, I'm afraid of—AAAHHHHHHH!"

Joe suddenly let out a terrified scream. A real one! They were being attacked by a giant sea creature!

Chapter 2

STARSTRUCK

"We're under attack by a sea monster!" Joe shrieked as a six-foot-tall starfish shoved him out of the way.

"Watch where you're going, kid. You stepped on my foot," the starfish grumbled, bending over to rub the bottom of a starfish-arm-shaped leg.

Frank grinned. "It's Seymour the Sea Star, the other new mascot!"

Joe giggled nervously. "I knew it was a costume. I was just testing you all to see if you'd believe it."

Frank rolled his eyes at his brother.

"Nice to meet you, Seymour!" Mira said.

"Yeah, yeah, that's me. Seymour, the overqualified giant talking sea star with two wasted degrees in marine biology. Woo-hoo." Seymour's costume had a big cartoon grin, but it didn't sound like the guy inside was smiling. "Just take a picture or something already so we can get the humiliation over with."

Apart from being six feet tall, having a goofy smiley face, and walking upright, Seymour looked just like a white starfish, with raised brown dots running down the center of each of its five arms. Each of the dots looked exactly like a giant chocolate chip.

"Seymour's a chocolate chip sea star. The species is called that because of the way the spines look on each arm," said Brady.

"The spines are used as a defense to scare predators away," Frank added quickly. He didn't want to be outdone by Brady.

"Huh, they look pretty tasty to me," Joe said.

"Is a sea star the same thing as a starfish?" Mira asked.

"A lot of scientists prefer the name 'sea star' because they're not actually fish—" Frank started to answer, but Brady cut in.

"They're echinoderms. That's a type of a sea creature that also includes sea urchins and sea cucumbers."

Joe's stomach grumbled. "Cucumbers? Is anybody else getting kind of hungry?"

"Chocolate chip sea stars are popular with home aquarists because of their unique appearance," Brady continued.

"They live in warm, shallow water in the Indian and Pacific Oceans, like the rest of the creatures in Tide Town," added Frank.

"If you two know so much, what do you need me for?" Seymour asked grumpily, trying to scratch his back against the wall. "What a waste of time. I should be running the show at Tide Town instead of Mouna. She's only got one degree. She should be the one stuck inside a stuffy starfish costume entertaining a bunch of brats like an aquatic clown at a kiddie convention."

"You're technically a sea star," Brady reminded Seymour.

"Well, I think your chocolate chips are cute." Mira gave one a squeeze. "You look like a giant starfish cookie!"

"That's just great. Really, really great. I've been reduced to a cookie." Seymour threw two of his five arms up in frustration. "That's the last straw. I'm not letting management get away with this."

The giant sea star with the smiley face tried to storm off, but his costume seemed to be stuck to the wall. He gave a few grunts and yanked himself free with a loud *POP*. When he stomped away, the kids could see rows of little, wiggling, pink-tubed feet with suction cups running along the back of the costume's arms, just like an actual sea star.

"I sure hope the real Seymour is less grouchy than its costumed counterpart," said Frank.

"Who knew a sea star could be so crabby?" Joe asked.

"Keep up, kids!" Ms. Klinger shouted back at Frank, Joe, Mira, and Brady.

They hurried to catch up to the rest of their classmates, and a few minutes later, the whole group followed their teacher past a hand-painted wooden sign pointing the way to Tide Town. When they stepped inside, there were a bunch of other kids already there, along with a few other teachers and parents.

Tide Town's walls were painted to look like a tropical beach, and there were even a few realistic-looking palm trees scattered around the room. Soothing wave sounds and seagull noises played from the speakers, adding to the beach vibe. Tanks along the walls were filled with different sea animals, but the main attraction was the huge, round pool in the center of the room.

When the class gathered around the pool, Frank and Joe made sure they were right up front. Looking down, they could see all kinds of cool creatures. Some of them were swimming around, like the sleek-looking spotted rays. Others were just chilling out, like the spiky sea urchins and a pair of bright orange sea stars. There were lots of rocks, making all kinds of nooks and crannies where other creatures were hiding too.

"Don't forget, anyone who writes down every one of the creatures living in Tide Town gets extra credit *and* an official Junior Marine Biologist badge," Ms. Klinger said to their group. "You have to get the list just right, though. Official Junior Marine Biologists always pay attention to detail."

"Consider it done, Ms. K!" Frank replied. "It will be just like deep-sea detecting."

Everybody at school knew that Frank and Joe loved to solve mysteries. Their dad, Fenton Hardy, ran a private investigation agency, so detecting ran in the family.

"I am so getting a badge," Brady said. "No one is better at identifying aquatic animals than I am."

A woman with braided brown hair wearing a button-down shirt waved to everyone from the other side of the pool. Her name tag said MAYOR MOUNA.

"Welcome to Tide Town, everyone!" she said, speaking into a small wireless microphone so the whole room could hear her. "My name is Mouna, and I'm the mayor of Tide Town. It's my job to introduce you to all the wonderful aquatic residents living in our touch pool."

"Hi, Mayor Mouna!" many of the kids called back.

"That's got to be the Mouna the Seymour mascot was angry at for getting the Tide Town job instead of him," Joe whispered to Frank.

When the chatter died down, Mayor Mouna

continued her introduction. "Tide Town is Bayport Aquarium's re-creation of a tide pool like the ones on the shorelines of the western tropical regions of the Pacific Ocean. Tide pools are the shallow, rocky pools of seawater that form when the tide recedes. There are lots of interesting creatures that call the pools home. Would you like to meet our residents?"

"Yes!" Frank and Joe shouted along with the rest of the kids.

"You can reach in and touch them gently on their backs with two fingers." Mouna reached into the pool to demonstrate and lightly touched a ray as it swam past. "Just remember, always be gentle. You probably wouldn't like it if someone bopped you on the head, and animals don't either."

Frank, Joe, and Brady all reached into the water to touch some of the creatures.

"Hey, look. It's Seymour the sea star!" Mira said from behind them, pointing to a chocolate chip sea star clinging to one of the walls. One of its chocolate-chip-armored arms was sticking up out of the water. "He's even cuter than the Seymour mascot, and a lot less crabby."

"How come his arm is out of the water? Don't they have to stay all wet if they live in the ocean?" one of the other kids asked Mouna.

"Oh, Seymour will be just fine," she replied. "You should never take sea creatures out of their habitat unless it's an emergency, but sea stars can survive out of water for a little while when they have to. It's a special adaptation they have so they can stay in the pools when the tide goes out and the cracks and crevices where they live are exposed to air."

"Sea stars have a special valve that they can close when they sense the water getting lower," Brady announced to Tide Town from beside Frank.

"That's exactly right!" Mayor Mouna said.

"Well done, Brady." Ms. Klinger smiled proudly.

Brady puffed his chest out and smirked at Frank.

"I knew that too," Frank mumbled under his breath.

"I hope to have a sea star of my own once I get my parents to buy me a fish tank," Brady told Mouna.

"I even know all about the water conditions they need to be happy living in an aquarium, like they are here."

"My twin sister, Avery, would love to have a chocolate chip sea star like Seymour so much," said Mira. "I wish I could take him home for her!"

"Would you like to touch one?" Mayor Mouna asked Mira. "All of our sea stars are super friendly."

"Yuck!" Mira jumped back from the pool and turned a little green. "I think Seymour is the cutest, but I'm not putting my hand in the water with a bunch of slimy creatures. My sister is the only Junior Marine Biologist in our family."

Tide Town was suddenly filled with a loud squawking noise, and it wasn't coming from the speakers. Mayor Mouna's face lit up.

"Penguins ahoy!" she said, pointing to the Tide Town entrance.

A whole bunch of real penguins were marching into Tide Town! With their black-and-white feathers, they looked almost like they were wearing tuxedos.

"Cool!" Joe said, giving Frank a high five.

"Say hi to the aquarium's colony of African penguins." Mayor Mouna waved to the funny-looking birds. They didn't wave back, but the Bayport Aquarium employee wrangling them did. "Benjamin is leading our daily Penguin Parade. They're on the way to their outdoor exhibit for feeding time." She pointed to the other side of the large room, where there was an arched doorway with a hand-painted driftwood sign beside it reading MORE EXHIBITS THIS WAY.

There was a buzzing by Frank's left ear, and when he looked up, a big, fat bumblebee flew by. "Huh," he said, watching the insect dip and dive through the air. "A bumblebee must have accidentally bumbled into the aquarium."

Frank wasn't the only one who saw the bee. So did some of the penguins! A few stopped to follow it back and forth with their heads.

"Penguins are incredibly playful, and they all have big personalities. Isn't that right, Benjamin?" asked Mouna.

"You said it, Mouna!" Benjamin turned back to the penguins. "Come on, girls and guys, let's get a move on. A fresh-fish feeding frenzy awaits!"

The bee buzzed away, and Benjamin continued marching, with most of the penguins following behind him. But one broke away from the parade to chase the bumblebee!

"Come back here, Lee!" Benjamin yelled.

Lee didn't listen, and he wasn't the only one. Some of the other penguins ran after him to join the pursuit. Suddenly there were penguins everywhere. It was a feathered free-for-all!

PENGUIN PANDEMONIUM

While Lee chased after the bee, some of the other penguins chased after Lee, and Benjamin chased after them all. Meanwhile, the rest of the penguins took off in five different directions, with Mayor Mouna racing after them. And it wasn't just the penguins that were out of control. Kids started running everywhere. Some tried to help herd the penguins, while others wanted to avoid the chaos. While Mouna and Benjamin ran around wrangling birds, teachers and chaperones were trying to wrangle the kids!

"They're headed our way!" Frank called out, pointing at the bee buzzing toward the touch pool, with Lee waddling after it in hot pursuit.

"It's coming to get me!" Brady shrieked, sprinting away from the touch pool and the runaway penguin.

"Please stay together, kids!" Ms. Klinger shouted. Joe and Frank could barely hear her over all the laughter, screaming, and squawking.

Now one of the birds was coming right at them! Joe and Frank leaped out of the way, just before Lee hopped up onto the edge of the touch pool and dove into the water with a splash.

Frank pushed himself up onto his knees and cautiously peered over the rail into the pool. "I don't think Lee cares that much about Tide Town's rules."

The penguin seemed to have forgotten all about the bee and was swimming around in circles, chasing frightened rays. It must have looked like fun, because three more penguins hopped in to join him!

It was a penguin pool party! None of the kids

jumped into the water, but many of them were laughing and giggling and chasing birds around the exhibit. Mayor Mouna, Benjamin, Ms. Klinger, and the rest of the adults looked horrified by the Tide Town turmoil. All except one.

Joe pointed at a man creeping through Tide Town with a sinister grin on his face. He was about six feet tall, with spiky hair and pointy eyebrows. He had on shorts, flip-flops, and a plain black T-shirt, so he didn't look like one of the aquarium staff or one of the teachers.

"I wonder what that guy's so smirky about."

The guy gave one last smug look at the mayhem before disappearing.

Frank shrugged. "I don't know, but this is pretty funny."

It took another ten minutes for the adults to get the penguins back in line and to settle the kids down.

"Sorry about that, folks." Benjamin chuckled nervously and looked back at the penguins. "Why do you guys have to make me look bad?"

Lee squawked something back at him, but it was in penguin.

Frank glanced down at his watch and his eyes went wide. "Ms. Klinger, it's almost ten o'clock. Can we follow the penguins and go see feeding time?"

"I don't trust those penguins." She gave a doubtful look at the parade waddling out of Tide Town. "But I did say you could, so just be careful. Those birds are as poorly behaved as some of my students!"

Frank and Joe marched behind the penguins all the way through another wing of the aquarium to an outdoor exhibit called the Penguin Palace. It had a rocky beach with a cave and a huge tank where the penguins could go swimming. It looked just like a real beach where penguins might live, only this one had balls and squeaky toys scattered all around. There were stairs leading down to a lower level, where a huge glass wall gave visitors a fish-eye view of the penguins swimming underwater. None of the birds were in the water at the moment, though.

They were all eagerly following Benjamin onto

the beach, where another employee was waiting with overflowing buckets of fresh fish.

"Hey, no shoving!" Benjamin scolded Lee as the rambunctious penguin pushed his way to the front of the line.

Kids gathered around to watch the second employee feed the penguins a variety of small fish and squid.

"Hmm, kind of makes me hungry for sushi," Joe said to Frank.

Benjamin picked up a beach ball and tossed it to himself. "They're a little distracted by lunch, but as some of you saw firsthand, penguins are super curious and playful animals. It's kind of like taking care of a colony of bird-shaped puppies and kittens! They even play with toys."

"And bumblebees!" Joe called out. Kids who'd been in Tide Town during the commotion started giggling.

"Thanks for reminding me." Benjamin chuckled, turning a little pink.

The boys watched the penguins eat and play

for a while longer before Frank suddenly turned to Joe.

"I was so distracted by the penguin pandemonium at Tide Town, I forgot to write down all the creatures in the touch pool for extra credit! I can't let Brady be the only one to get a Junior Marine Biologist badge!"

"Let's get you that badge, bro," Joe said, turning and marching back toward the door leading inside. "See ya later, penguins!"

Frank and Joe were halfway back to Tide Town when Brady ran up behind them.

"Hey, Frank. Did you see the kaleidoscope jaguar shrimp hiding under the coral in the touch pool?"

"The who-what shrimp?" Joe asked.

Frank looked confused too. He knew a lot about marine biology, but he hadn't heard of the shrimp either.

"The kaleidoscope jaguar shrimp," Brady said. "It's a super-rare relative of the peacock mantis shrimp. Bayport Aquarium is one of the only aquariums in the world to have one. It's really colorful, like the inside of a kaleidoscope, and it can also change colors to look like its environment. Maybe that's why you didn't see it. I guess I just have really good eyes when it comes to spotting sea life." He tapped his blue-framed glasses.

"I have good eyes too," Frank grumbled. "I was just distracted."

Brady shrugged. "I'm going to check out Shark Row. See you guys later."

"I wish I'd seen that kaleidoscope jaguar shrimp for myself the first time," Frank said after Brady had left. "At least now I know it's there so I can add it to the extra-credit list. Ms. Klinger said we had to write down *every* creature in Tide Town. If Brady hadn't told me about it, I might have missed out on seeing a cool shrimp *and* getting that badge!"

When they made it back to Tide Town, the exhibit was entirely empty except for Mayor Mouna and her aquatic citizens.

"It must be between tour times," Joe said. "Maybe you can ask Mayor Mouna if there are any other hidden creatures, so you don't miss anything."

"Hi, Mayor Mouna!" Frank called.

Mouna didn't seem to hear him. She was too busy staring into the touch pool, scanning the rocks as she chewed on her fingernails.

"What's wrong?" Joe asked as he and his brother came to her side.

Mouna didn't answer right away. She ran to the other side of the touch pool, clearly searching for something. Finally she looked up at Frank and Joe.

"He's gone!"

"Who's gone?" Frank stared down into the pool. He definitely didn't see the kaleidoscope jaguar shrimp, but there was another creature that he didn't see either.

"Seymour the chocolate chip sea star!" Mouna cried. "He's missing from the tank!"

Chapter 4

TIDAL TURMOIL

"Are you sure he's not there?" Joe saw plenty of rays, some urchins, a few shrimp, and even some other sea stars, but none of them were white with chocolate-chip-shaped lumps on their arms. It looked like Mayor Mouna was right. Seymour the sea star was gone!

Frank examined a mound of coral in the middle of the touch pool. "Could he just be hiding under something?"

"I've looked everywhere!" Mouna cried. "I

checked all his favorite hiding spots, but Seymour is one of our most outgoing residents. He's almost always out and about, crawling around the tank."

Joe gave his brother a knowing look. "I think this calls for the clue book."

"The what book?" asked Mouna.

Joe held up his notebook so she could see. "The clue book! Frank and I are the top kid detectives in Bayport, and this book is where we write down the five *W*s at the start of every mystery."

"And a missing chocolate chip sea star sure sounds like a mystery to me," Frank said.

Mouna glanced from Joe's notebook back to Frank. "What are the five *W*s?"

"*Who*, *what*, *where*, *when*, and *why*. As in, *who* did it? *What* did they do? *Where* did it happen? *When* did they do it? And *why* did they do it? Those are the five questions we need to answer to crack any case."

"*What* and *where* are easy." Joe pulled out a pen and started writing. "Seymour at Tide Town."

"*When* isn't too hard either," said Frank. "Seymour

was here during our tour, so we know he had to have gone missing sometime between then and now. Do you remember when you last saw him and when you first realized he wasn't there anymore?"

"Well, he was right there on the side of the pool when the Penguin Parade showed up." Mayor Mouna pointed to the spot where they'd all seen Seymour during their first visit. "I'm not sure after that. I always check on all our residents after a tour, just to make sure everyone's okay after the kids leave. Your tour ran late because of the penguins, so I didn't get a chance until the next tour was over. That was about ten minutes ago, and I realized he was gone right before you got here."

"The penguins arrived at about nine forty-five, right before we left for penguin feeding time at ten, and it's ten thirty-five now, so he had to have gone missing between nine forty-five and ten twenty-five." Joe jotted the times down in the clue book.

Frank gave a quick look around at the rest of the exhibit. "Could he have climbed out of the touch pool and wandered off on his own?"

Mouna shook her head. "None of the creatures have before. They don't have any reason to. Sea stars can stay out of water for short periods of time, but they only do it when they really have to, like when the tide gets too low."

"I guess that brings us to *who*," Frank said.

Mouna gasped. "You think he was star-napped?!"

Joe glanced into the water and gulped. "Is it, um, possible one of the other Tide Town residents ate Seymour?"

"No way," Mouna replied. "We make sure all the animals in the same tank are friends with one another. Someone must have taken him!"

"Did you notice anyone acting suspiciously during either of your tours?" Frank asked.

"No one could have taken him while I was watching! I pay close attention to all the kids to make sure everyone is being nice to the animals. If someone tried to take one of them out of the pool, I'd notice it for sure."

Joe snapped his fingers. "It must have happened while you weren't watching!"

"But I always watch—" Mouna's mouth dropped open. "Oh! You mean the Penguin Parade!"

"Yup. You were helping Benjamin chase the penguins around while Lee ran after the bumblebee."

Joe crossed out *Between 9:45 and 10:25* and wrote *Between 9:45 and 9:55*. "The crime had to have been committed during the ten minutes when everyone was distracted by the runaway penguins."

"Now it's back to *who*." Frank stared down at the

Who:
What: Seymour
Where: Tide Town
When: between 9:45 40:25
            9:45 - 9:55

Why:

clue book page. "Everyone who was here during our tour could be a suspect. There were tons of kids, along with a bunch of teachers and parents too. How do we narrow it down?"

"Why in the world would anyone want to take an innocent sea star?" Mouna asked.

"Good question." Joe circled the word *Why* in his clue book. "In the detective biz, *why* is what we call motive."

Mouna thought for a minute. "Well, it doesn't happen very often, but guests have been caught trying to steal fish from other exhibits for their home aquariums."

Frank narrowed his eyes. "I can think of one fishless home aquarium enthusiast who was here when the penguins were running everywhere."

Joe jabbed his pen in the air. "Brady! He even said he wanted a sea star of his own."

Frank nodded. "I think we have our first suspect."

Joe was writing Brady's name next to *Who* when they heard shouting on the level below Tide Town.

Joe, Frank, and Mouna all ran out of the exhibit and looked over the railing to see what was happening in the rain forest on the floor below.

Two of the aquarium's mascots were shaking their costume fins and arms and yelling at each other. The one yelling the loudest had five arms decorated with large, chocolate-chip-shaped lumps.

"You can keep that silly suit on for the rest of your life for all I care! I'm going to take my breaks whenever I want to!" Seymour the Sea Star mascot shouted at Reggie the Ray.

"Wow. He's even more unhappy about wearing that costume now than he was when I stepped on his foot on the way in," Joe said.

Mouna buried her face in her hands. "Tide Town's opening day is a total disaster. Our mascots are fighting in front of the kids, and I lost our star attraction!"

"You know what? Having to wear the mascot costume wasn't the only reason Big Seymour was so grouchy." Frank looked from the fighting mascots back to Mayor Mouna. "He was complaining

that you got to be Tide Town's mayor instead of him."

"That's right!" Joe quickly flipped the clue book back open. "Brady isn't the only *who* with a *why*. There's another shady character with a motive for taking Seymour—the other Seymour!"

FISH FIGHT

"We'd better go talk to him and see if he had anything do with Little Seymour's disappearance," Frank said to Mouna. He ran for the stairs leading down to the rain-forest exhibit, with Joe right on his heels.

It was a lot warmer in the rain forest, and the air was sticky with moisture from all the jungle plants and the waterfall trickling down the wall. Joe could see tanks full of scary-looking piranhas, trees filled with colorful birds, and even a fake sloth dangling from one of the branches. What he didn't see was a guy in a Seymour costume. "We must have just missed him."

"Reggie the Ray is still here." Frank pointed at the mascot in the ray costume. "Maybe we can get some useful information from him."

Joe walked up to Reggie and tugged on one of the ray's fins. "Excuse me, Mr. Ray. Is it okay if we ask you a few questions?"

Reggie turned around and looked down at him and Frank. "Sure thing. I can tell you all about the different creatures in our aquarium."

Reggie's voice sounded a little shaky, like the mascot was still angry from the fight and trying not to show it. Joe was surprised when he heard Reggie speak, because it sounded like a woman inside the costume.

"Sorry, Miss Ray!"

"You can just call me Reggie," they said with a laugh. "What would you like to know about our residents?"

"We were hoping you could tell us about the six-foot-tall one in the sea star costume you were just arguing with," Frank said.

Reggie looked down at their fins. "Oh no. I'm sorry you heard that. We're supposed to be setting a good example for the guests."

"I think that ship already sailed," Joe said. "He yelled at us earlier. But we think he might be up to something fishier than just grumbling about his fishy costume."

Reggie gasped. "Pat yelled at some of our guests? I'm going to have to report that. Ditching his shift is one thing, but we're the aquarium's mascots! The most important part of our job is to make sure kids like you are having a good time."

"'Pat' is Big Seymour's real name?" Frank asked. "And that's why you were arguing? Because he walked out on his shift?"

Reggie nodded their giant ray head. "We were mobbed, and he just took off without anything, leaving me to entertain a whole lobby full of kids all by myself. That's not fair to me or the guests. Just because he doesn't like wearing his costume doesn't give him permission not to do his job."

"He ran off suddenly, huh?" Joe shot a look at Frank. They both knew what their next question had to be. "What time did he leave?"

Reggie thought for a second. "I think it was about nine thirty-five, maybe."

"That fits our timeline!" Frank looked back at Joe. "Pat would have had just enough time to slip out of his costume and make it from the lobby up to Tide Town!"

"What happened at Tide Town?" Reggie asked.

Frank dodged the question, not wanting to reveal too much about the case until he knew more. "What does Pat look like when he's not dressed like a giant sea star?"

"He's got spiked hair and his eyebrows are kind of arched. How come?"

"Spiky hair and pointy eyebrows?" Frank said. "That matches the description of the smirky guy we saw sneaking through Tide Town during the penguin stampede. He was there at the same time the real Seymour went missing. Pat could have been stealing away with a stolen sea star!"

Joe held up the clue book. "He was *where* and *when*, and he has a *why*. I think we could have our *who*!" He added Pat's name to the suspect list.

"What?" Reggie asked. "You're saying someone stole Seymour from Tide Town? And you think it was Pat?"

"Someone sure did." Frank nodded, a serious look on his face. "Pat even told us he wasn't going to let the aquarium get away with passing him over for the Tide Town mayor job and making him wear the Seymour costume. Nabbing the real Seymour could have been his idea of revenge."

"Let's track him down and see if we can get him to confess to—" A drop of liquid splatted down onto Joe's shirt before he could finish. "Ack! What was that?"

A second drop hit Reggie on the head, and a third left a wet splotch on Frank's sneaker. All three looked up.

Someone was peering over the railing of the level above. They were crouching down like they didn't want to be noticed. The only things the boys could make out were the person's eyes and the top of their head. That, and the leaky fish-tank-themed lunch box dangling over the rail.

Frank scowled. "Brady."

Brady's eyes went wide when he realized he'd been spotted. More liquid splattered down onto Frank and Joe as Brady yanked the leaking lunch box back over the rail and raced down the hall away from Tide Town.

THE ELECTRIC SLIDE

"When a suspect takes off running after a crime, it usually means one thing," Joe said. "They're guilty of something."

Frank stared at Brady's back as he ran. "I bet I know what he's guilty of. Brady told everyone he wanted a sea star of his own, and what better place to hide it than a lunch box decorated to look like a fish tank?"

"He knew sea stars could be taken out of the

water and the right water conditions to keep them in too," Joe added. "He could have planned the heist in advance and filled his lunch box with a plastic bag full of aquarium water to turn it into a portable starfish tank. That would explain the dripping!"

Frank could still see Brady's neon-green shirt moving along the rail of the level above. "Let's go after him!"

"There's a shortcut to get upstairs at the other end of the rain forest!" Reggie pointed their fin down the hall. "Don't let him get away with it!"

Frank and Joe took off running. There was another stairway at the rain-forest exit, just like Reggie had said. Behind the stairs was a dark, roped-off corridor with a sign that said UNDER CONSTRUCTION—AQUARIUM STAFF ONLY. Luckily, the brothers weren't going that way. Halfway up the stairs, Joe glanced down and saw Mira sneaking past the sign. She had a Bayport Aquarium gift bag in her hand and was looking around nervously, like she didn't want anybody to see her. Joe thought about mentioning her strange behavior to Frank, but right then they had bigger fish to fry.

Under Construction-
Aquarium Staff Only

"There he is!" Frank shouted when he reached the landing.

Brady was one of the fastest kids in school, and if it hadn't been for Reggie's shortcut, the Hardy brothers would have lost him right away. Even with the shortcut, he had a big lead, sprinting through the door of an exhibit at the other end of the hall labeled WEIRD AND WONDERFUL WORLDS.

Joe leaped over one of the little puddles Brady's leaking lunch box had left behind. "Careful not to slip, bro!"

"That poor sea star! The way that lunch box is bouncing up and down, it must be dizzy." Frank's eyes widened as they entered a long, curved hallway lined with displays full of fantastic creatures. "I wish we could stop to check out all these cool tanks."

Joe grabbed his brother's arm to keep him from slowing down. "No time for sightseeing, dude. Brady's getting away!"

They ran past swirling rainbows of fish and alien-looking sea anemones, ancient-looking sturgeon the size of sharks, floating clouds of jellyfish that lit up with pink and blue bioluminescence, and all kinds of other weird and wonderful sights.

"Excuse us! Aquatic emergency! Marine detectives coming through!" Joe called out as they weaved their way past the exhibit's surprised guests.

Frank pointed at Brady's neon-green shirt disappearing around the corner ahead. "We're losing him!"

By the time Frank and Joe rounded the corner, Brady was closing in on the exit sign at the end of the exhibit. His lunch box bounced against his leg as he ran, sending drops of liquid flying into the air.

Frank pumped his fists to make himself run faster. "According to the map, this leads to three other exhibits. If Brady makes it out that door, we may never find him."

There was one last tank at the end of the Weird and Wonderful Worlds exhibit—the electric eels—and Brady had almost reached it.

"He's going to give us the slip!" Joe shouted.

But just at that moment, Brady's sneaker landed in a puddle from his leaking lunch box. He tried to catch his balance by pinwheeling his arms and swinging the lunch box in circles, but it was no use. He slid right off his feet onto his behind and skidded to a stop next to the electric eel tank. A fat, gray electric eel watched with beady little eyes as Brady's lunch box popped open, spilling its contents onto the floor.

"He gave himself the slip!" Joe said as the boys closed in.

With Brady on his behind, they had no problem catching up to him. He frantically tried to pick up the spilled contents of his lunch box, but Joe was quicker.

Frank glared down at Brady while Joe looked for the lost sea star. "Done in by your own leaky lunch box."

"Something's leaking all right, but I don't see Seymour." Joe tossed aside a PB&J sandwich, a handful of carrots, and a nearly empty, very sticky thermos.

Frank eyed the lemonade-colored puddle left at the bottom of Brady's lunch box. "Um, that doesn't look very much like seawater."

"Seawater?" Brady squinted up at them and

adjusted his crooked glasses. "Why in the world would I have seawater in my lunch?"

"Hmm . . ." Joe dipped his finger into the liquid, and then he gave it a lick to confirm his suspicion.

MARINE MISCHIEF

"Wow!" Joe grabbed the thermos and took the last gulp. "That's delicious!"

"Hey, that's my dad's famous homemade lemonade!" Brady said.

Joe handed the empty thermos back to Brady. "Compliments to the chef."

Brady shook the thermos and frowned. "You drank it all."

"Chasing you made me thirsty, and you spilled

most of it, anyway." Joe pointed to the puddle Brady had slipped in. "In case you didn't notice, your thermos has been leaking all over the aquarium."

Frank picked up the lunch box and examined it for himself. "You're sure there isn't a sea star in here?"

"If Brady took Seymour, he didn't hide him in his lunch box," Joe said. "Our theory about him turning it into a portable aquarium doesn't hold water."

"Take Seymour?" Brady's eyes widened. "Why would you think I took Seymour?"

Frank scowled at him. "Someone did, and you're the one who said you wanted a sea star for your home aquarium."

"But I don't have a home aquarium yet. And even if I did, I would never steal an animal from the Bayport Aquarium." Brady crossed his arms. "I'm an ethical home aquarist. The illegal tropical fish trade causes tons of harm to the ocean. I only want sustainable, legally sourced specimens for my tank."

"Then why did you run when we caught you spying on us?" Joe asked.

Brady looked guiltily down at his hands. "No reason."

"No reason, huh?" Frank narrowed his eyes. "Maybe we should ask Ms. Klinger what she thinks."

Brady gasped. "Don't, please!"

"Then spill," said Frank. "And by 'spill,' I mean 'talk,' because you already spilled all your lemonade."

"Well, I may have not been totally honest with you about seeing that rare kaleidoscope jaguar shrimp in the touch pool," Brady said without looking Frank in the eyes.

"Why would you lie to me about seeing one of the creatures in Tide Town?" Frank asked.

"Because it doesn't really exist. I kind of made it up to get you to write down the wrong thing and mess up the extra credit so I would score higher."

"I knew you were guilty of something!" said Frank.

"It just wasn't sea star snatching," Joe said.

"It's extra-credit sabotage!" Frank pounded his fist into his other hand.

"I'm sorry, Frank." Brady looked up and bit his lip.

"I know it was wrong. I just wanted Ms. Klinger to think I was the school's best Junior Marine Biologist."

"I'm not ready to accept your apology quite yet. Just because you confessed to trying to sink my assignment doesn't clear you of sea-life lifting," Frank said. "You still could have used the runaway Penguin Parade as a distraction to grab Seymour from the touch pool while Lee was splashing around."

"But it couldn't have been me!" Brady shuddered. "I'm afraid of penguins!"

"That's right! When *who*ever was taking the *what* from the *where*, Brady was running the other way to flee from the penguins!" Joe concluded. "As soon as the penguins ran for the touch pool, Brady flew the touch-pool coop!"

Frank grimaced at the memory.

"Um, now I think we're the ones who are guilty." Frank held his hand out to help Brady up. "We shouldn't have falsely accused you of felony fishiness."

While Frank pulled Brady back to his feet, Joe pulled out the clue book and crossed Brady off the suspect list. There was only one name left.

COSTUMED CULPRIT

"Pat," Joe said. "He's back to being aquatic enemy number one."

"Who's Pat?" asked Brady.

"The real name of the grouchy guy in the Seymour costume," Frank replied.

"He was there at the *where* and *when,* and he has a *why,*" Joe said.

Brady stared at Joe like he was speaking a different language. "What?"

"*What* is Seymour," Joe replied, holding up the clue book.

"Seymour is a chocolate chip sea star." Brady shook his head and sighed. "I know you're not a Junior Marine Biologist in training like Frank and me, but you really should pay better attention, Joe."

Frank giggled.

"I know what kind of animal Seymour is! But he's also our *what*." Joe pointed to the clue book page with the five *W*s. "*Who, what, where, when,* and *why* are the questions we need to answer to solve the mystery of the stolen sea star. We thought *who* was you, but now we think it's Pat. *Where* is Tide Town. *When* is during the penguin pool party. That's when Seymour was taken. And *why* is the motive for the crime."

"Revenge," Frank declared. "Pat was angry at the aquarium for making him wear the Seymour mascot costume instead of letting him be mayor of Tide Town, where the real Seymour lived."

"We saw him after he ditched the starfish suit, sneaking through Tide Town at the time of the crime. He was back in costume arguing with Reggie the Ray a few minutes before we ran after you. Who knows where he went after that." Joe looked around Weird and Wonderful Worlds and out the exit at the other exhibits. "It's a big aquarium. Pat could be anywhere. How do we track him down to interrogate him?"

Brady's eyes lit up. "I know where he is! At least I know where he was going. I saw him heading toward the food court when I was watching you guys."

Joe slammed the clue book shut and looked at Frank. "Let's go, bro!"

"Go get him and bring the real Seymour home!" Brady yelled after Frank and Joe as they marched out the door.

They were closing in on the food court when they saw the six-foot-tall, chocolate-chip-spotted sea star surrounded by kids in front of a nearby souvenir stand. Two of the mascot's five arms were crossed over his chest as a group of little kids tugged at his chocolate chips.

Frank narrowed his eyes at the costume's huge,

friendly smiley face. "If Pat is really smiling, I bet it's a villainous smile."

Joe looked the mascot up and down. "I wonder if he has the real Seymour hidden in his costume or if he stashed him somewhere else."

"Let's go find out." Frank rubbed his hands together and marched toward the souvenir stand.

"Hey, Seymour," Joe called. "Remember us?"

Seymour looked down at the brothers. There was no way to tell, but Joe had a good hunch the guy behind the mask was frowning.

"Yeah, the klutz and the know-it-all. How could I forget?" He sounded just as crabby as the first time they'd met him.

Joe had to try really hard not to stomp on his foot again. "We know even more than you think . . . Pat."

Pat took a surprised step backward. He shook the little kids off his chocolate chips. "Scram, brats. I'm closed for business." He waited for the kids to scatter before turning back to Joe. "How do you know my name?"

"Oh, we know a lot more about you than that,"

said Frank. "Like how you left Reggie the Ray alone and ditched your shift to sneak off to Tide Town."

"Have you been following me?" The giant sea star's voice cracked, and he backed farther away.

"We also know what you did when you got there."

Joe took another step closer. Pat tried to back up even more, but he bumped into one of the huge windows looking out over Bayport Harbor. There was nowhere left for him to go, which was exactly where Joe and Frank wanted him.

"I bet sabotaging Tide Town made you feel really good after getting passed over for the mayor job," Frank said.

This time, Pat was the one who surprised them—by laughing. "Benjamin's penguins sabotaged Tide Town, not me. It was pretty funny, though. It's the aquarium's own fault for letting a beginner like Mouna run an important exhibit instead of choosing me."

"Sure, blame the birds," Joe said. "Pretty clever to use the penguins as a distraction, but we know what you were really doing when Benjamin and Mouna were busy chasing them around."

"Stealing a helpless sea star is pretty low"—Frank pointed a finger at their costumed suspect—"even for someone as grouchy as you."

"Stealing a sea star?" Pat paused to glance down at his own mascot costume. "What are you talking about? I don't want this ridiculous outfit. They made me wear it."

Joe looked at Frank. Pat sounded genuinely confused.

"We don't think you stole the costume," Joe said. "We think you stole Seymour!"

"Stole Seymour? I *am* Seymour!" Pat raised two of his sea star arms into the air.

"You're Big Seymour. We mean Little Seymour," Frank said.

"You mean the actual sea star?" Pat scratched his costumed head. "What would I want to steal a sea star for?"

"For revenge," Joe said. "We saw you sneaking through Tide Town without your costume on at the exact same time the real Seymour went missing."

"I don't know anything about that," Pat insisted.

"I was passing through Tide Town on my way to the aquarium offices to tell my boss what I thought about being stuck with the mascot job."

"We saw the shady look on your face. It was obvious you were up to no good," Frank said.

"Okay, sure. Maybe I was happy things went wrong for Mouna, but I didn't cause them to go wrong. I was just lucky enough to be in the right place at the right time. I didn't even know the real

Seymour was stolen until you told me just now. Do you really think I'd go talk to my boss with a stolen sea star in my pocket?"

Joe thought it over before replying. "That would be pretty gutsy. But how do we know you actually went to see your boss and aren't just making that up to give yourself an alibi?"

"I can't believe I'm defending myself to a couple of nosy kids."

Pat sighed and lifted off the head of his costume. He was definitely the same spiky-haired guy with the villainous-looking pointy eyebrows they'd seen in Tide Town. He stuck one of his sea star arms out at Joe.

"Unzip my hand so I can get out my cell phone."

Before unzipping his hand, Joe looked around to make sure there were still plenty of people nearby in case the guy tried anything funny. Once Pat's hand was free, he reached into his costume and fished around for a minute before pulling out his phone.

"We have to scan our employee ID card anytime we go into the office." He tapped one of the icons on his phone and started to scroll. "There's an app that records all the time stamps to show when everyone goes in or out of any of the employees-only areas. Here."

He shoved the phone in front of the boys' faces. The screen had the official Bayport Aquarium logo at the top, with Pat's name and the times he'd gone in and out of the office.

"He went in at nine fifty-six," Frank said. "That's right after we saw him in Tide Town. And he left fifteen minutes later. That means he went straight to the back office, like he said." Frank looked up from the phone and stared Pat down. "That still doesn't prove you were talking to your boss. You could have gone in there to hide Seymour before anyone caught you."

"Nice try, kid, but the office is always full of people. You can ask anyone who works here, and they'll tell you the same thing. My alibi is watertight."

"He was also wearing shorts and a T-shirt when we saw him," said Joe. "I don't think Seymour could have fit in his pocket, and it would have been hard to hide a sea star under his shirt while talking to his boss." He sighed and pulled out the clue book. "I hate to say it, but I think he's telling the truth."

A second later, Pat was crossed off the suspect list.

Pat put the head of his Seymour costume back on and trudged off, muttering to himself. "I really hate this job."

Frank stared at the blank space under Pat's crossed-out name. "Both our theories were wrong, and now we're out of suspects!"

Frank and Joe both racked their brains trying to figure out what they might have missed. A minute later, Frank snapped his fingers.

"You know what? Brady wasn't the only one in our group who said they wanted to take Seymour home!"

Joe gasped as it hit him too.

"That's right! There's one more suspect we overlooked. Mira said she wanted to bring Seymour back to her twin sister, since Avery couldn't be here to see him in Tide Town."

Frank nodded. "Mira had a motive, and she was there when the crime took place."

"That's not all," added Joe. "When we were chasing Brady, I saw her sneaking around in a roped-off area. She could have been hiding Seymour, or even stealing *more* creatures for Avery!"

"We'd better go find Mira before she has a chance to take any more," Frank said.

They didn't have to search far. Mira was in the food court by the bakery stand.

"Oh no!" Frank pointed at the object in Mira's hand. "We're too late!"

Frank and Joe looked on in shock as Mira lifted Seymour . . . and started to eat him!

EDIBLE EVIDENCE

"Talk about hiding the evidence!" Joe wailed. "Mira is eating it! Even I don't get that hungry!"

Frank and Joe sprinted into the food court, waving their arms.

"Put Seymour down!" Frank shouted.

Mira froze with the sea star in her mouth and gawked as the boys ran toward her. She looked almost as surprised as they did. It wasn't until they got closer that they realized why.

There were cookie crumbs tumbling out of her mouth. And chocolate on her teeth. And . . .

"Um . . ." Frank tapped Joe's shoulder and pointed to the cookies in the bakery stand's glass display case. "I don't think she's eating Seymour the chocolate chip sea star. I think she's eating a Seymour-shaped chocolate chip cookie."

Joe examined the glass case. There was a whole row of identical Seymours. Next to them was a little sign that said FRESH-BAKED COOKIES.

"The sea star she's eating is a red herring!"

Mira coughed out a mouthful of cookie. "Ew! Why would I be eating a real sea star? And what's a red herring?"

"A red herring is a mystery clue that leads in the wrong direction," Frank said. "Someone stole the real Seymour from Tide Town, and we thought it might have been you."

"Yuck!" Mira said, turning a little green again. "Seymour is cute, but I wouldn't touch any of those creatures if you gave me a million dollars. I can't believe you thought I'd eat one!"

Joe scratched his chin. "I guess Mira was one of the only kids who didn't want to reach into the touch pool. It would have been hard to steal a sea star without actually touching it."

"Um, if you didn't steal Seymour, how come Joe saw you sneaking into an employees-only area?" Frank asked.

"Well, I know we're not supposed to have cell phones. . . ." Mira looked around to make sure no one was listening. "But my mom gave me one for emergencies, and, well . . . it's not really an emergency, but I really wanted to call Avery to see how she was feeling. I was afraid if Ms. Klinger saw me, I'd get in trouble. Don't tell anyone, okay?"

"You're sure you didn't steal Seymour?" Joe asked.

"I actually did plan to bring Seymour home for Avery. . . ."

Joe and Frank tripped over each other trying to lean in closer. This was the big clue they'd been waiting for!

"Just not the real one. I got her a whole box of sea

star cookies *and* a stuffed Seymour toy."

Frank's shoulders slumped as Mira pulled a large stuffed chocolate chip sea star out of her aquarium gift bag.

"That's not the confession I was hoping for."

"Sorry, guys. I really hope you find whoever did it. Seymour is too cute to be star-napped!"

Mira walked off, nibbling on her Seymour cookie.

"I don't even need to open the clue book to know we're really out of suspects now." Joe looked around the food court. "Mira's Seymour cookie did make me kind of hungry, though."

"How can you think of food at a time like this? What about the real Seymour?" Frank asked. "We still have a mystery to solve!"

"Detecting is harder on an empty stomach." Joe rubbed his grumbling belly. "I can barely think, surrounded by all this yummy food."

Frank's own belly rumbled back. "Well, I'm kind of hungry too. I guess we can talk about the case while we eat."

They looked around at the options. The food

court had lots of different types of foods, but that wasn't all it had. There was also a wall with a bunch of TV screens showing live cams of different exhibits so you could watch the animals while you ate. One of them had an underwater shot of the sharks swimming around Shark Row, and another showed Penguin Palace. The penguins on the screen were playing with a stuffed fish toy of their own. Next to the screens were framed pictures of some of the exhibits' star attractions, including a frighteningly large snaggletooth shark named Smiley and their old friend, Lee the penguin.

Joe looked from the picture of Lee to the ice-cream stand. A sign hanging from the ceiling above it advertised bird-shaped Penguin Pops.

"Now, that looks like a tasty penguin," he said, marching over to get one for himself. "Decision made!"

Joe bought one for Frank, too.

"Look! It has a paper wrapper instead of plastic." Frank pointed to a tiny smiling turtle logo with the words 100% RECYCLABLE, COMPOSTABLE,

AND BIODEGRADABLE printed on the Penguin Pop's label. "As a Junior Marine Biologist in training, I know that a lot of regular plastic trash ends up in the ocean, where it can hurt sea creatures."

"Sweet! It's tasty-looking and fish-friendly, too." Joe tore off the wrapper and took a bite out of the penguin's fudge-frosted noggin.

"I feel like a better detective already," he said through a mouthful of Penguin Pop. "Now, who else could have possibly stolen Seymour, and why?"

Frank's eyes lit up as he watched a drop of Joe's ice cream drip off the penguin and fall onto the floor.

"You were right about eating being good for detecting! I think your ice-cream pop may have just solved the mystery!"

THE HARDY BOYS—and
YOU!

DO YOU KNOW WHAT HAPPENED TO SEYMOUR THE CHOCOLATE

chip sea star?

Think like a Hardy Boy to crack the case. Write your answers down on a piece of paper. Or just turn the page to find out!

1. Frank and Joe ruled out Brady, Pat, and Mira as suspects. Who else could have taken the sea star from the touch pool?

2. Can you think of another way the sea star could have disappeared if none of the suspects took it?

3. When Frank saw Joe eating the Penguin Pop, he thought of a new clue they hadn't written down. Can you think of any clues they might have missed the first time?

4. Frank and Joe got excited when they found out that the Penguin Pop had a fish-friendly paper wrapper instead of plastic. Can you think of other ways to use less plastic and help keep the ocean clean?

Chapter 10

RISING STAR

"What if our *who* is also a *what*?" Frank asked, jumping up and down.

"Huh?" Joe looked from Frank back to his Penguin Pop. He had no clue how his ice cream was a clue, but if he didn't eat it fast, it would be a melty mess.

"It didn't pop into my head until I saw your Penguin Pop drip onto the floor. . . . Brady wasn't the only one dripping when they left Tide Town." Frank pointed at the framed animal portraits on the wall by the live cam of the penguins playing with their toy. "We've been trying to figure out which person had a reason to take Seymour, but the biggest trouble-maker at Tide Town isn't a person at all."

Joe thrust his Penguin Pop into the air. "It was a bird!"

"We'd better make a beeline for the penguin exhibit."

Frank took off running, with Joe right behind him. They had just passed Tide Town when they saw Brady in front of a nearby octopus tank, drawing one of the eight-armed creatures in his sketchbook.

"Brady!" Frank yelled.

Brady threw his arms up in the air. "I didn't do anything, I swear!"

"It's not you we're after this time," said Frank, skidding to a stop in front of the octopus tank. "We do need to borrow your lunch box, though. It's for a good aquatic cause."

"As long as you bring it back, I guess that's okay." Brady picked his fish-tank-themed lunch box off the floor and held it out to Frank.

"Deal!" Frank grabbed the lunch box and sprinted for the exit.

"Penguins straight ahead!" Joe shouted as they burst through the door leading to the outside exhibits.

The penguins from the live cam were still playing with their stuffed fish toy when the boys reached Penguin Palace. Mischief-maker Lee stood on the exhibit's tallest rock, squawking down at them. Frank and Joe grabbed on to the railing and scanned the rocky beach.

"I don't see anything up here," Frank said, leaning over to get a closer look.

One of the penguins waddled past them to the water's edge and dove in.

"I think that one has the right idea. Let's get a penguin's-eye view of what's under the water."

Joe led the way down the steps to the underwater part of the exhibit, where visitors could look through the glass at the penguins swimming around. There were more toys underwater, but it wasn't the colorful plastic rings that got the boys' attention. A strange, five-armed toy was slowly climbing up the glass.

Frank jabbed his finger at the tank. "One of these toys is not like the others!"

"Seymour!" Joe shouted, running up to the glass in front of the chocolate chip sea star.

"What's all the commotion about?" said a voice from behind them.

"Benjamin!" Joe turned around and spotted the penguin keeper. "Your star penguin stole Mouna's star sea star!"

Benjamin saw Seymour climbing up the glass and gasped. "Lee did that?"

"He must have mistaken Seymour for a fun toy when he was splashing around in Tide Town and carried him back here to the penguin exhibit," Frank said. "With you and Mouna busy chasing the other penguins, it would have been easy for him to grab one of the creatures without anyone noticing."

Benjamin held his face in his hands. "Oh boy. I'd better get Seymour out of there and back to Tide Town right away."

He ran to a door that said AQUARIUM STAFF ONLY and opened it with his ID badge. He reappeared a couple of minutes later on the beach, wearing a wet suit. Frank and Joe watched through the underwater window as he dove into the tank and gently pulled Seymour from the glass.

"He's getting a free lift back to the surface! Let's go meet them!" said Joe. He led the way up the stairs.

They got there just as Benjamin poked his head out of the water.

"I'd better lift him out of the water slowly so he has time to adjust," Benjamin said. "Poor Seymour's already been through a lot today!"

"We can take it from there," Frank said, opening Brady's lunch box. All that was left inside was the leaky thermos. He took it out and held the empty lunch box over the rail for Benjamin. "If you fill this with water, we can carry it back to Mouna so you don't have to leave the penguins."

"Good thinking! These penguins get into enough trouble even when I'm watching them. Who knows what they'd do on their own!" Benjamin grabbed the lunch box and scooped water into it. "It's a quick trip to Tide Town, and Seymour seems to have gotten used to the penguins' water just fine." He placed Seymour inside and closed the lid, then handed the lunch box to Joe.

"Brady's fish-tank lunch box really does make a great portable fish tank." Joe examined the container. "It's a little leaky, but we don't have far to go."

"Thanks, guys!" Benjamin called after Frank and Joe as they hurried back to the entrance. "You're real aquarium heroes. Seymour could have been lost forever if you hadn't found him!"

Benjamin wasn't the only happy Bayport Aquarium employee.

"Seymour!" Mouna shouted a few minutes later when Frank and Joe walked into Tide Town and popped open the lunch box.

She carefully lifted the sea star out and put him back into the touch pool with the other Tide Town residents.

"That's the last time we're going to let the penguins parade through Tide Town, that's for sure," she said when the Hardys told her how Lee had mistaken Seymour for a toy and smuggled him back to the penguin exhibit.

Joe pulled the clue book out one last time and filled in the final two *W*s.

"*Who?* Lee the penguin. *Why?* Sea stars are fun!"

"It's time for me to write something down too," Frank said, pulling out a notebook of his own. "My extra-credit list of Tide Town creatures!"

"Hey, Frank," Brady said from the Tide Town entrance. He was holding up the page of his sketchbook where he'd written down his list. "I was thinking maybe we could work together and compare notes. I mean, if you want to. That way, we're both sure to get Junior Marine Biologist badges."

Frank smiled. "You got it, partner! It's your lunch box that gave me the idea for how we could rescue Seymour, so we're kind of working together already. It makes sense for us to team up on the extra-credit investigation, too."

Joe grinned and threw an arm around each of them. "The tide sure has turned on this case!"

HELP DECODE CLUES AND SOLVE MYSTERIES WITH THE THIRD-GRADE DETECTIVES!

The Clue of the
Left-Handed Envelope

The Puzzle of the
Pretty Pink Handkerchief

The Mystery of the
Hairy Tomatoes

The Cobweb Confession

The Riddle of the
Stolen Sand

The Secret of the
Green Skin

Case of the Dirty Clue

Secret of the
Wooden Witness

The Case of the
Bank-Robbing Bandit

The Mystery of the
Stolen Statue

FROM ALADDIN
KIDS.SIMONANDSCHUSTER.COM